LITTLE RED WAGON

Katie Nix

In the month of October, on a colorful fall day,
Jonathan went out with his little red wagon to play.
"I'm off on a journey!" he said with a smile.
"To find what makes my heart full, I'll walk a good mile!"

Now down that winding road Jonathan strolled and he strolled,
And the wheels on that wagon they rolled and they rolled.
He took a deep breath, and he sang a sweet song,
And hoped that his journey would not be too long!

And as Jonathan traveled along that day,
He saw an elephant coming his way.
So big was that elephant, and Jonathan so small,
But that wouldn't stop them from having a ball!

"3, 2, 1...1, 2, 3...come Mr. Elephant, won't you ride along with me?
Though we are different, great friends we will be."
So the elephant hopped in and joined in Jonathan's song
As the little red wagon bumped joyfully along.

And as Jonathan and his friend traveled along that day,
They saw a mouse coming their way.
So quiet was that mouse, and Jonathan so loud,
But their special bond would stand out from the crowd.

"3, 2, 1...1, 2, 3...come Mr. Mouse, won't you ride along with me?
Though we are different, great friends we will be."
So the mouse hopped in and joined in Jonathan's song
As the little red wagon bumped joyfully along.

And as Jonathan and his friends traveled along that day,
They saw a giraffe coming their way.
So tall was that giraffe, and Jonathan so short,
But they could still lean on one another for support.

"3, 2, 1...1, 2, 3...come Mr. Giraffe, won't you ride along with me?
Though we are different, great friends we will be."
So the giraffe hopped in and joined in Jonathan's song
As the little red wagon bumped joyfully along.

And as Jonathan and his friends traveled along that day,
They saw a turtle coming their way.
So slow was that turtle, and Jonathan so fast,
But that wouldn't stop them from having a blast.

"3, 2, 1...1, 2, 3...come Mr. Turtle, won't you ride along with me?
Though we are different, great friends we will be."
So the turtle hopped in and joined in Jonathan's song
As the little red wagon bumped joyfully along.

And as Jonathan and his friends traveled along that day,
They saw a pig coming their way.
So dirty was that pig, and Jonathan so clean.
But the two of them together would be the
best of friends you've ever seen.

"3, 2, 1...1, 2, 3...come Mr. Pig, won't you ride along with me?
Though we are different, great friends we will be."
So the pig hopped in and joined in Jonathan's song
As the little red wagon bumped joyfully along.

Then suddenly Jonathan stopped and had a grand thought,
As he dreamed of the happiness in his heart he had sought.
He looked back at his friends piled high to the sky,
And he said to himself, "How blessed am I?"

And this is where Jonathan's journey fondly ends,
For his heart was full from the love of his friends.

The End

This book is dedicated to my son, Jonathan Matthew, who
was born on October 6, 2015 with a complex and rare combination of
congenital heart defects (HLHS/IAS). Jonathan underwent multiple
open heart surgeries in his first few months of life at Riley Hospital for
Children in Indianapolis, Indiana; he is currently expected to undergo
at least two more. *Little Red Wagon* is symbolic of his heart journey
and the family and friends that have supported him along the way.

For Jonathan, my little heart warrior...

Made in the USA
Middletown, DE
22 January 2018